THE REAL POOP ON PIGEONS!

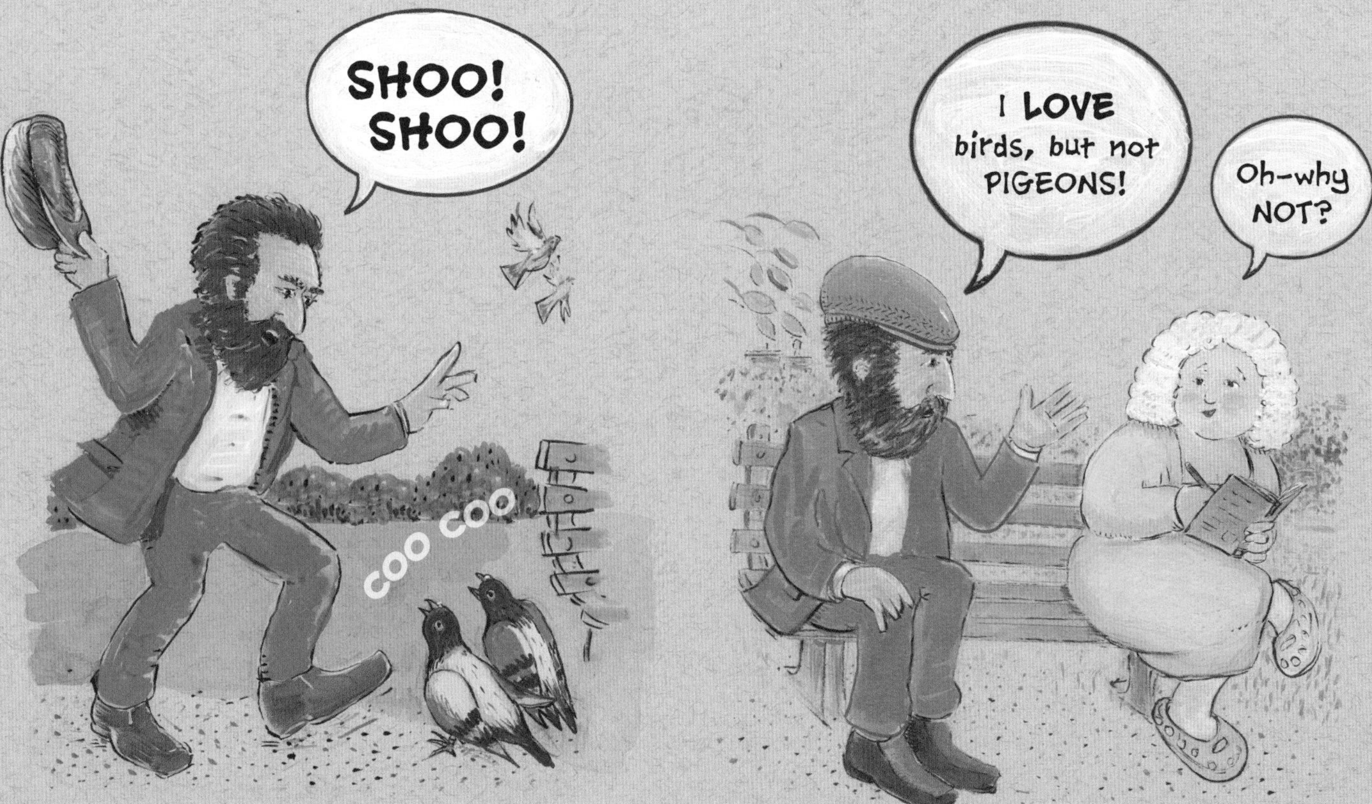
SHOO! SHOO!
COO COO
I LOVE birds, but not PIGEONS!
Oh-why NOT?

A TOON BOOK BY

KEVIN McCLOSKEY

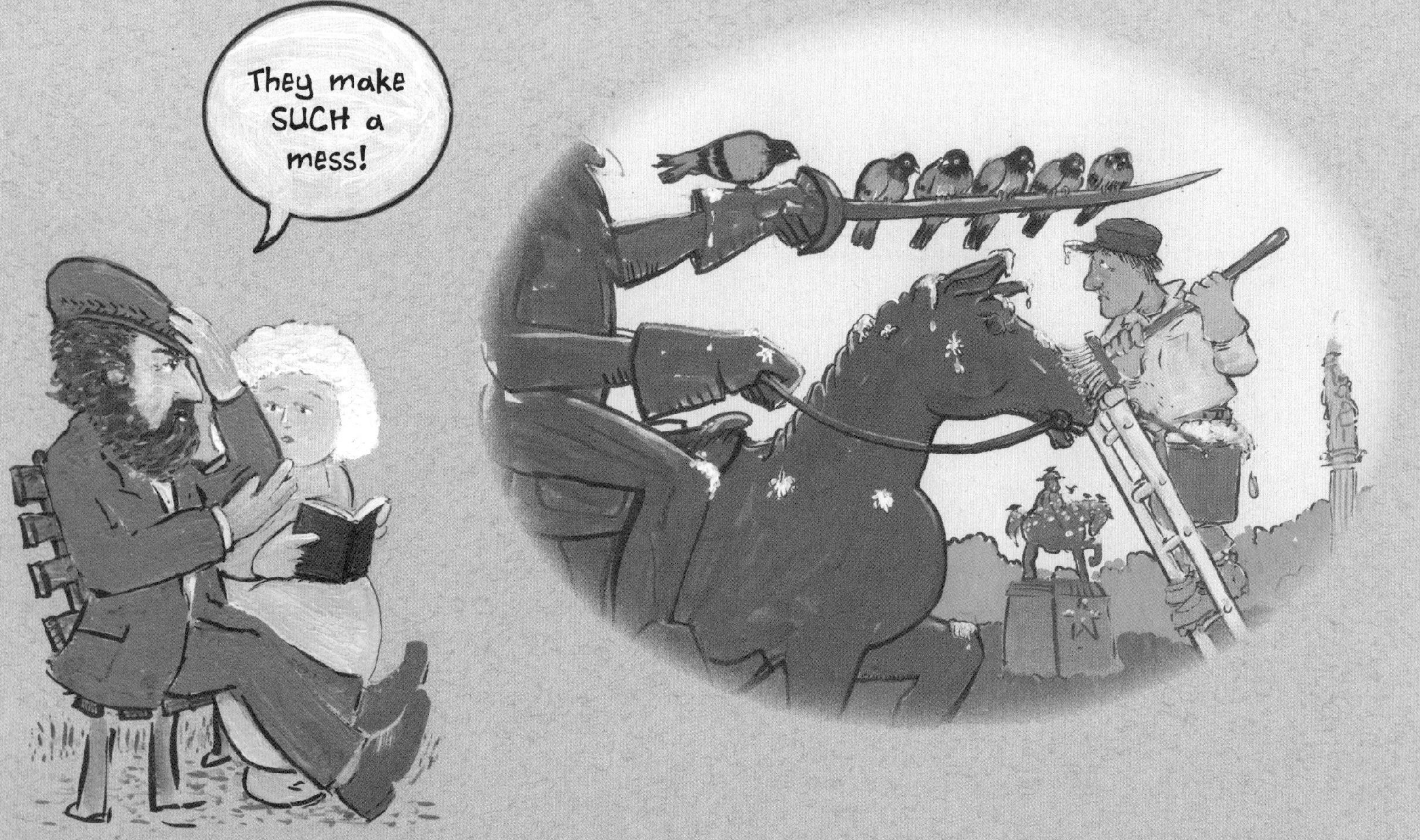
They make SUCH a mess!

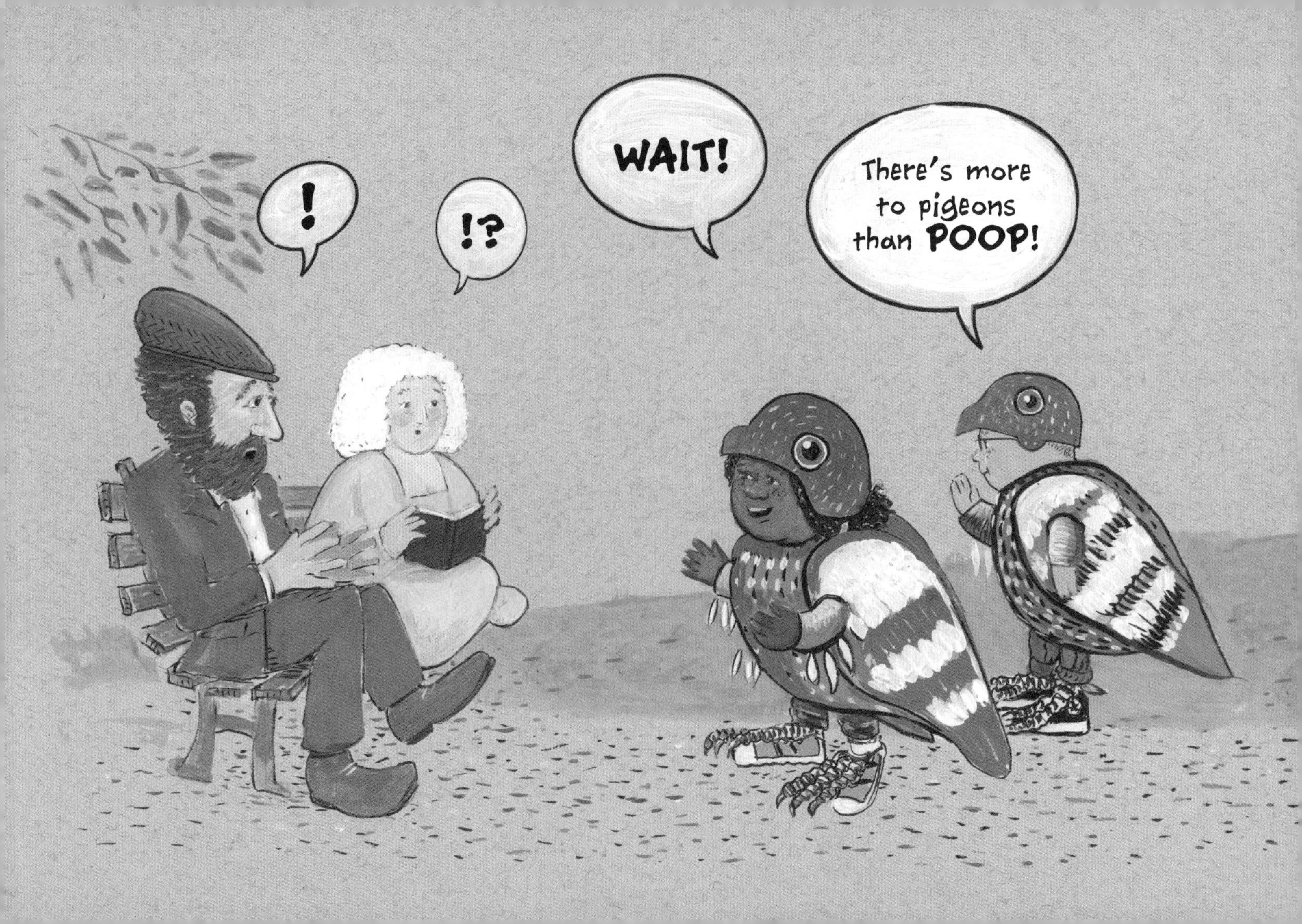
!
!?
WAIT!
There's more to pigeons than POOP!

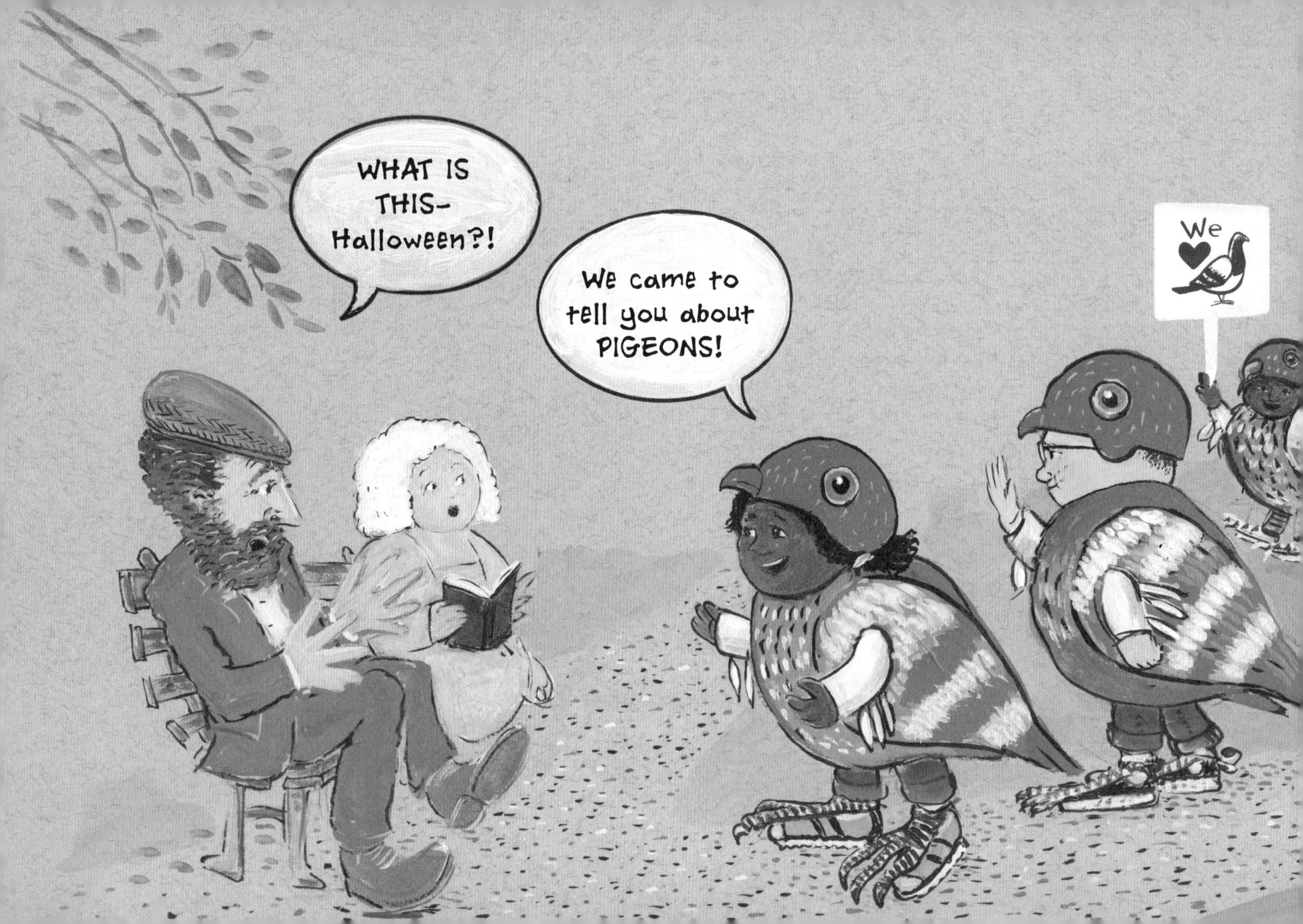
WHAT IS THIS- Halloween?!
We came to tell you about PIGEONS!
We ♥

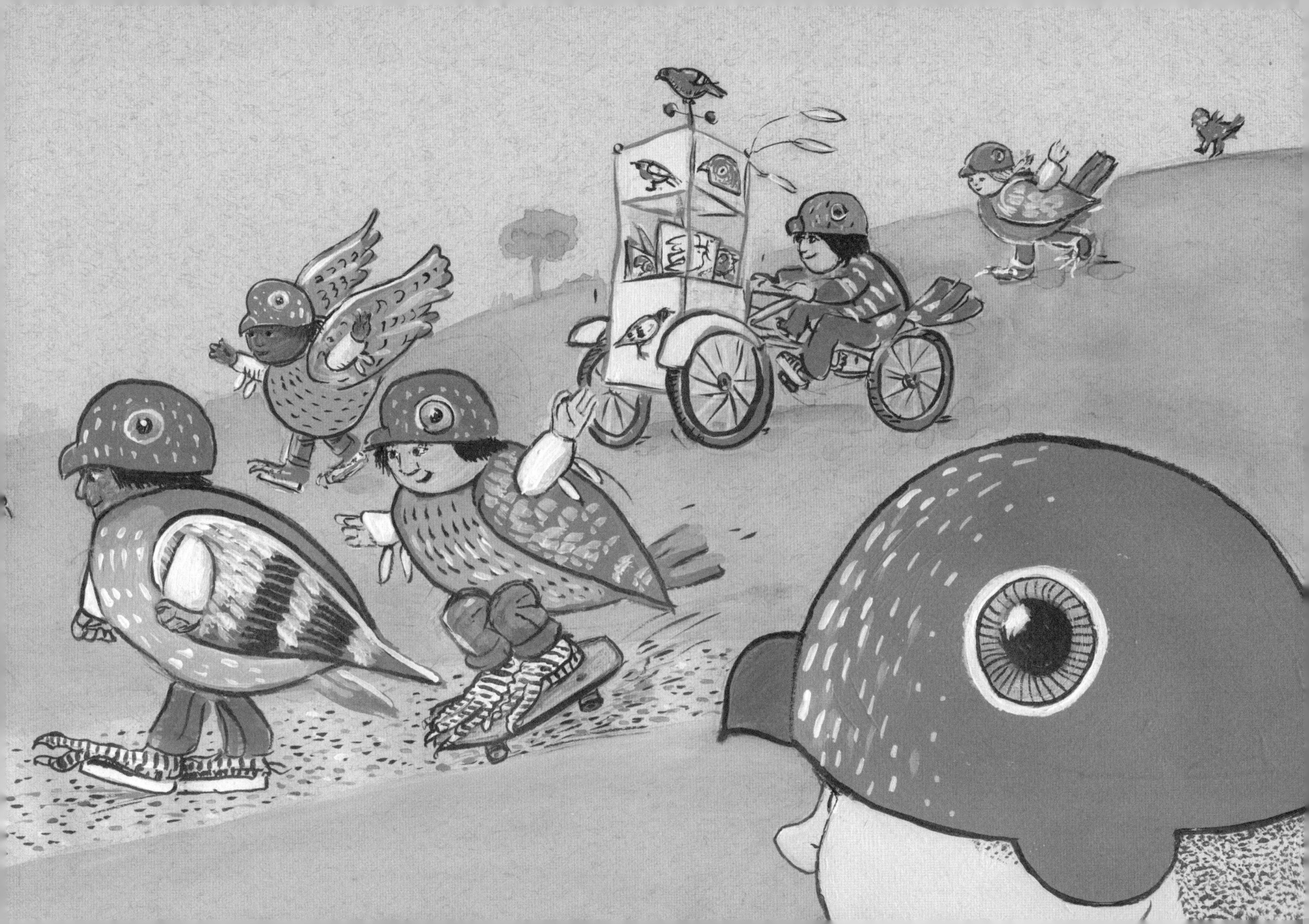

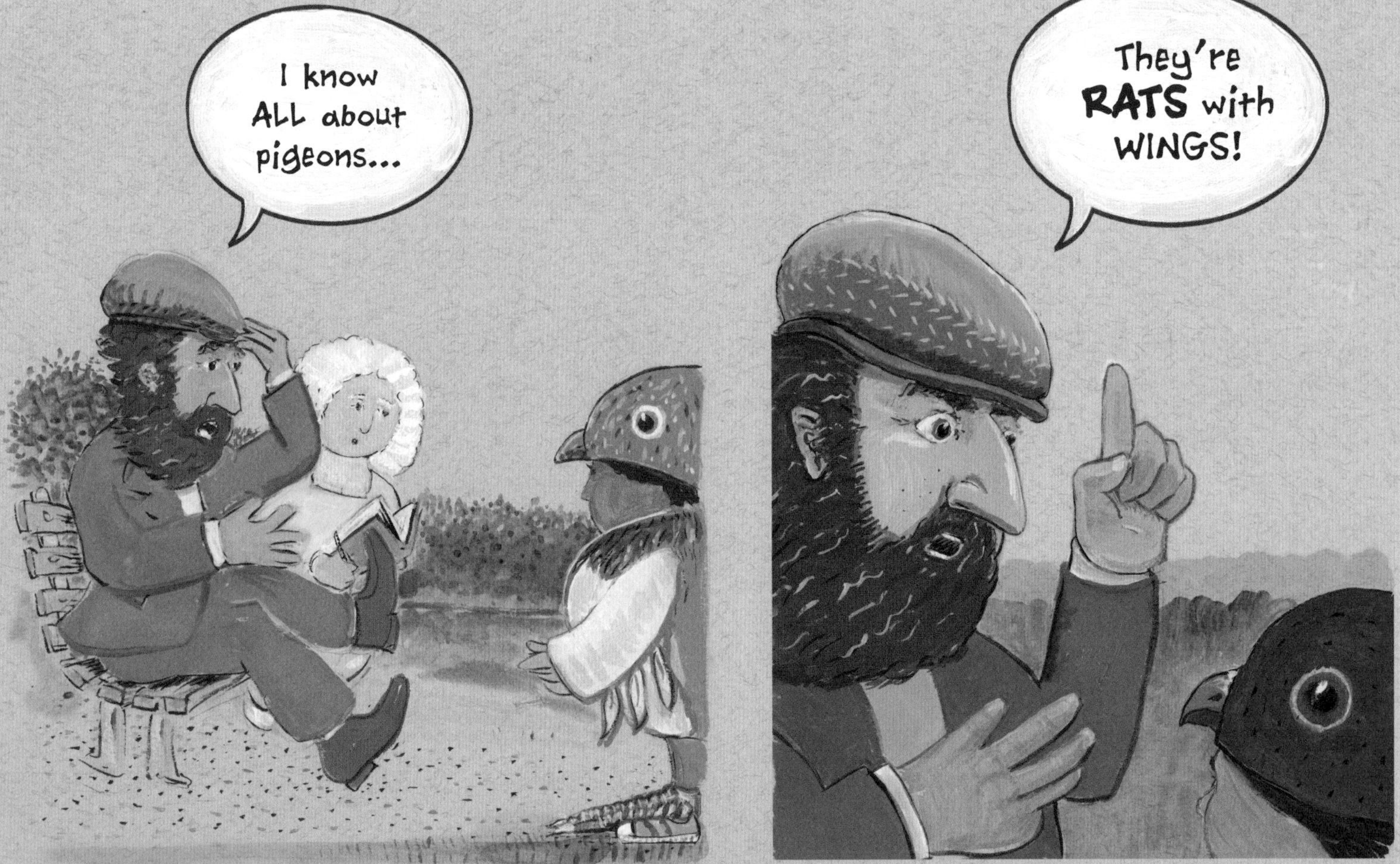
I know ALL about pigeons...
They're RATS with WINGS!

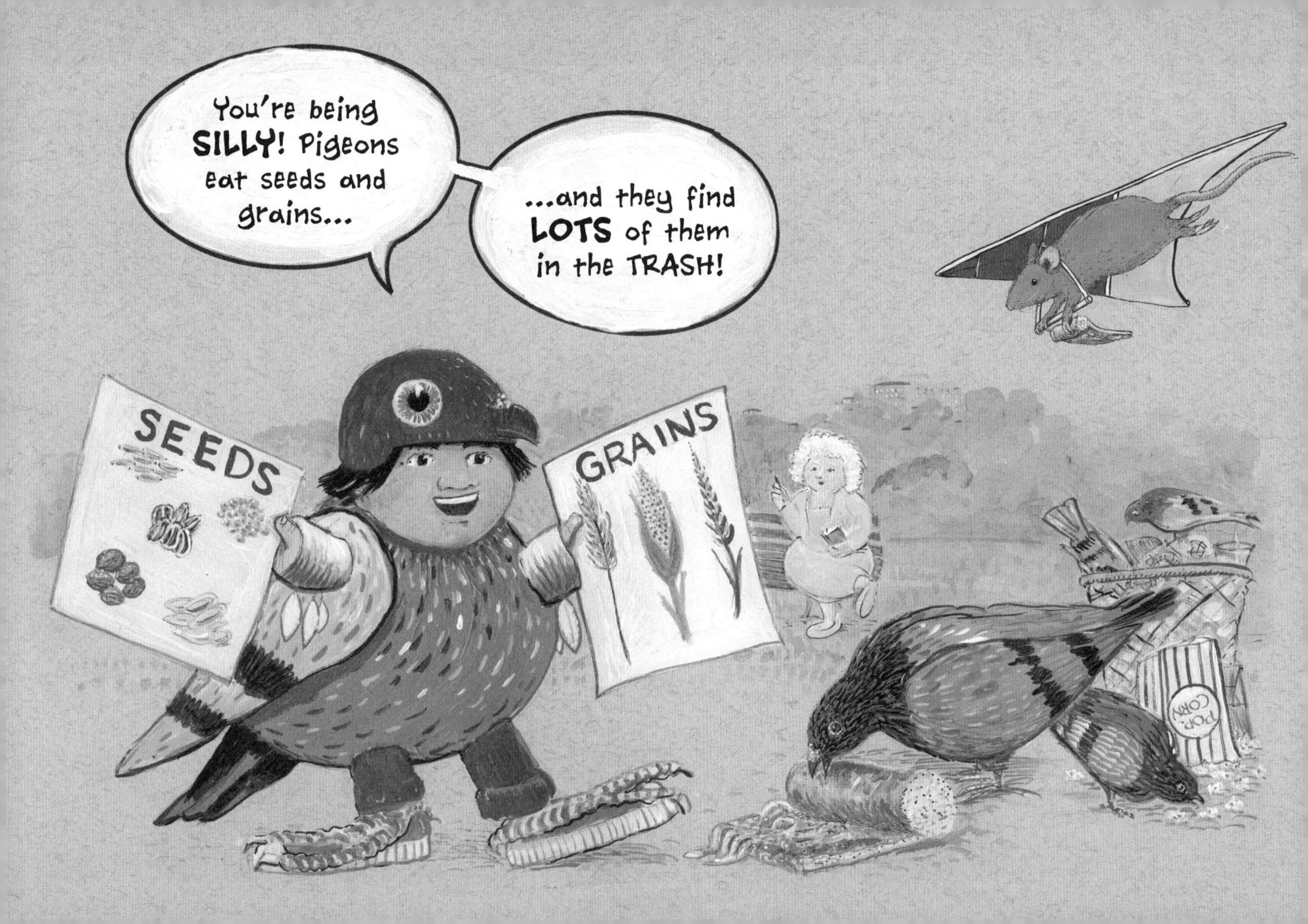
You're being SILLY! Pigeons eat seeds and grains...
...and they find LOTS of them in the TRASH!
SEEDS
GRAINS
POP-CORN

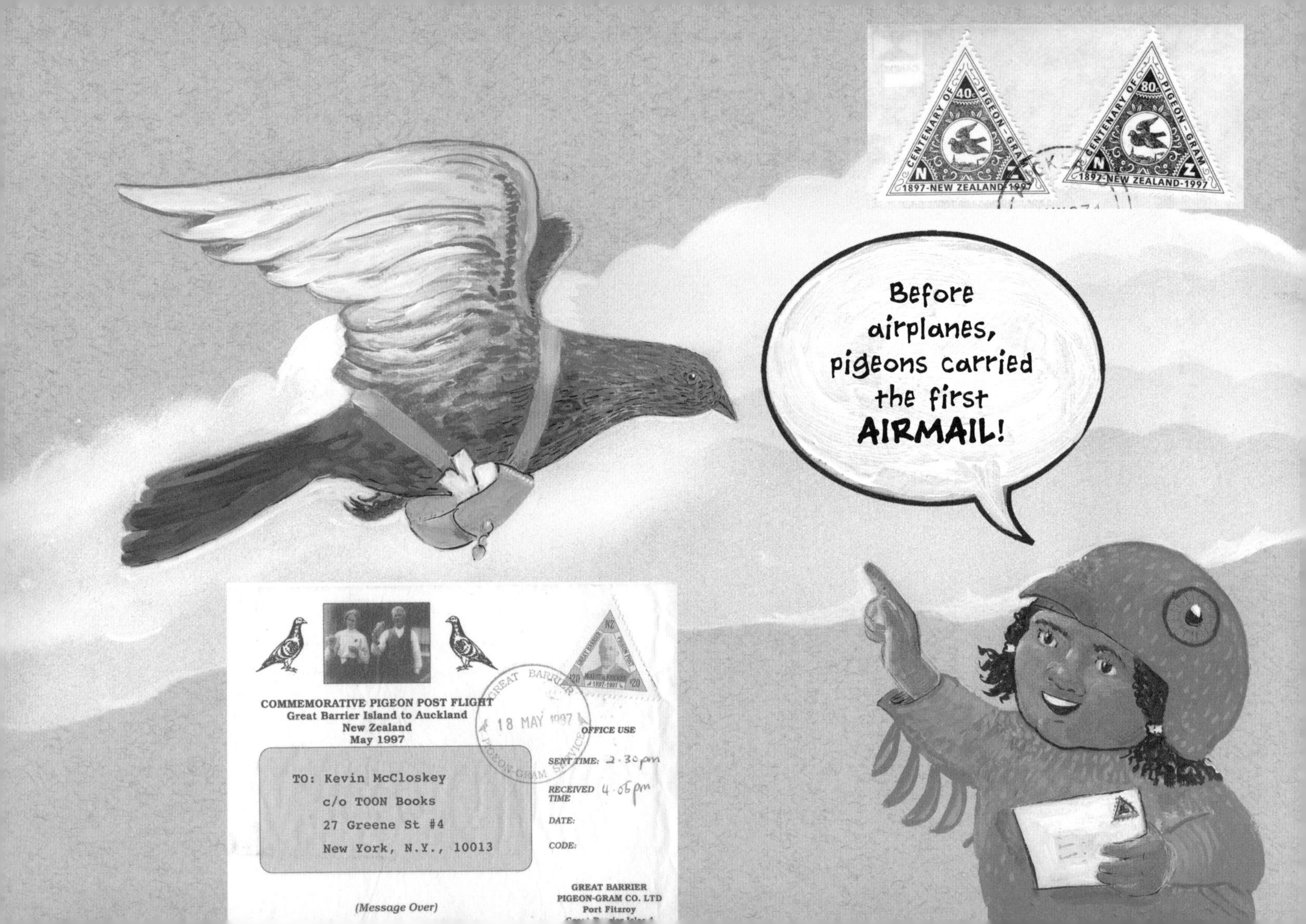

CENTENARY OF PIGEON-GRAM
40c
N Z
1897-NEW ZEALAND-1997
CENTENARY OF PIGEON-GRAM
80c
N Z
1897-NEW ZEALAND-1997
Before airplanes, pigeons carried the first AIRMAIL!
COMMEMORATIVE PIGEON POST FLIGHT
Great Barrier Island to Auckland
New Zealand
May 1997
GREAT BARRIER
18 MAY 1997
PIGEON-GRAM SERVICE
OFFICE USE
SENT TIME: 2.30pm
RECEIVED TIME 4.05pm
DATE:
CODE:
TO: Kevin McCloskey
c/o TOON Books
27 Greene St #4
New York, N.Y., 10013
(Message Over)
GREAT BARRIER
PIGEON-GRAM CO. LTD
Port Fitzroy

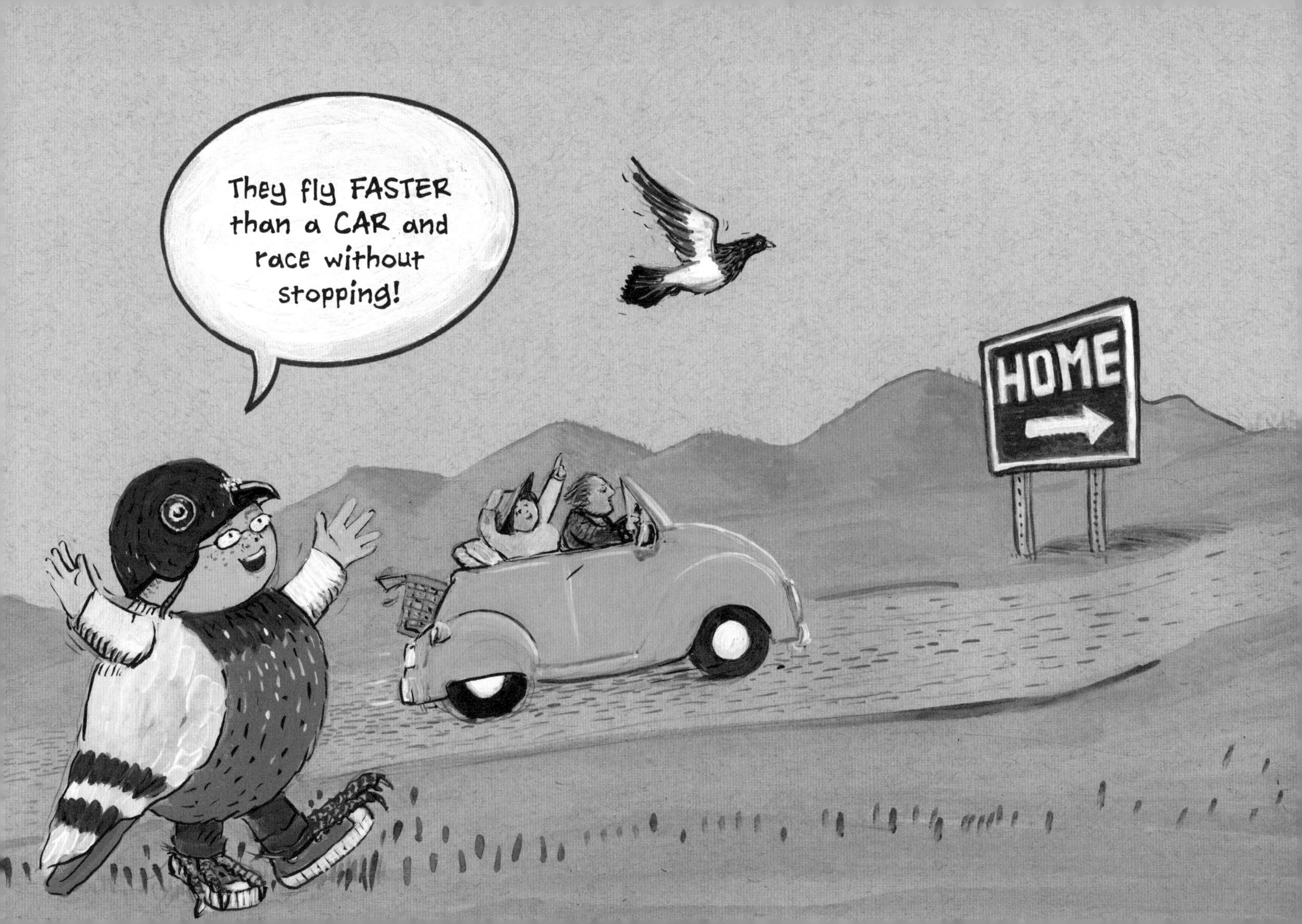
They fly FASTER than a CAR and race without stopping!
HOME

PIGEONS ARE IN THE SAME FAMILY AS DOVES.

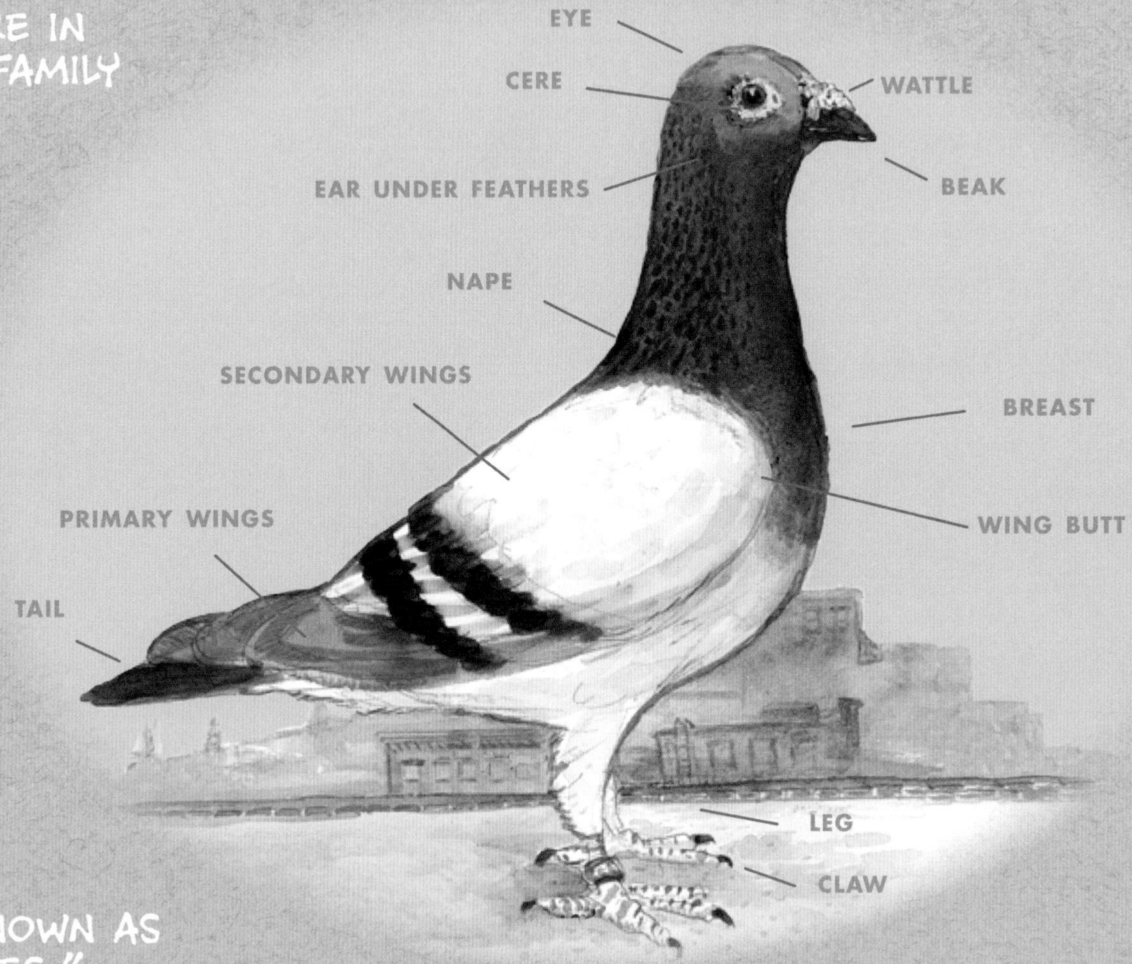
EYE
CERE
WATTLE
EAR UNDER FEATHERS
BEAK
NAPE
SECONDARY WINGS
BREAST
PRIMARY WINGS
WING BUTT
TAIL
LEG
CLAW

THEY'RE KNOWN AS "ROCK DOVES."

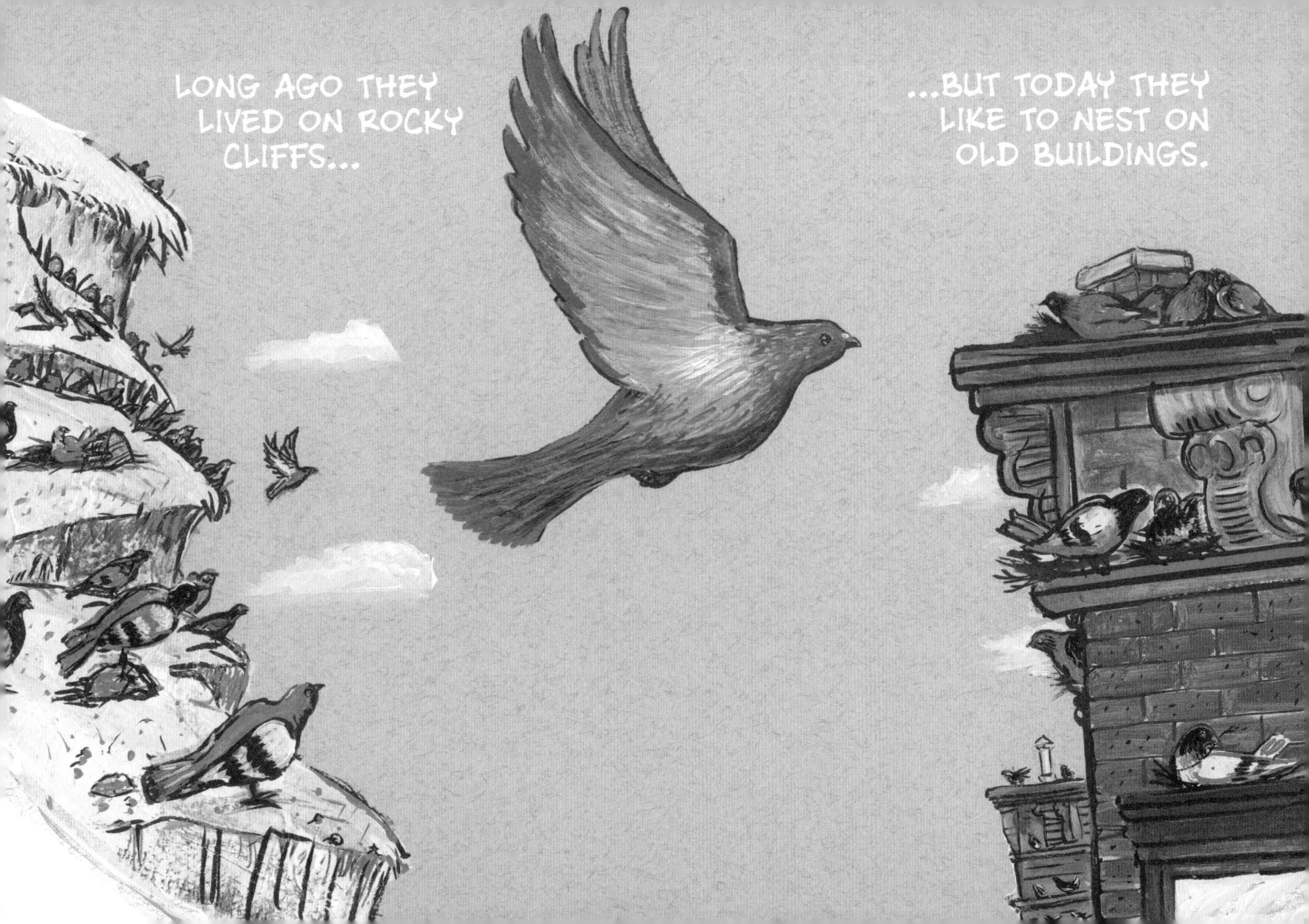
LONG AGO THEY LIVED ON ROCKY CLIFFS...
...BUT TODAY THEY LIKE TO NEST ON OLD BUILDINGS.

WHEN TWO PIGEONS MAKE A FAMILY, THAT'S CALLED **MATING.**

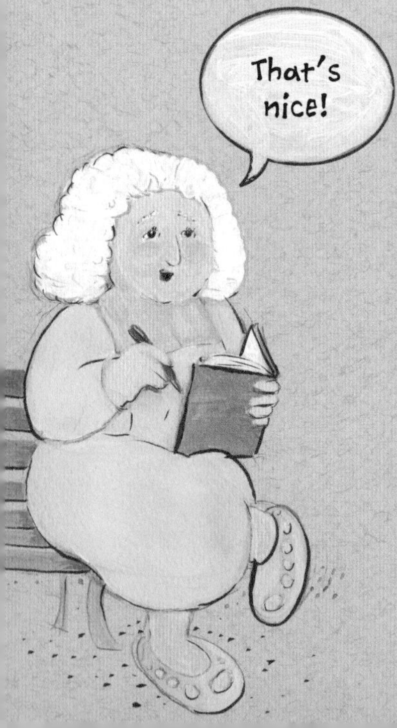
That's nice!

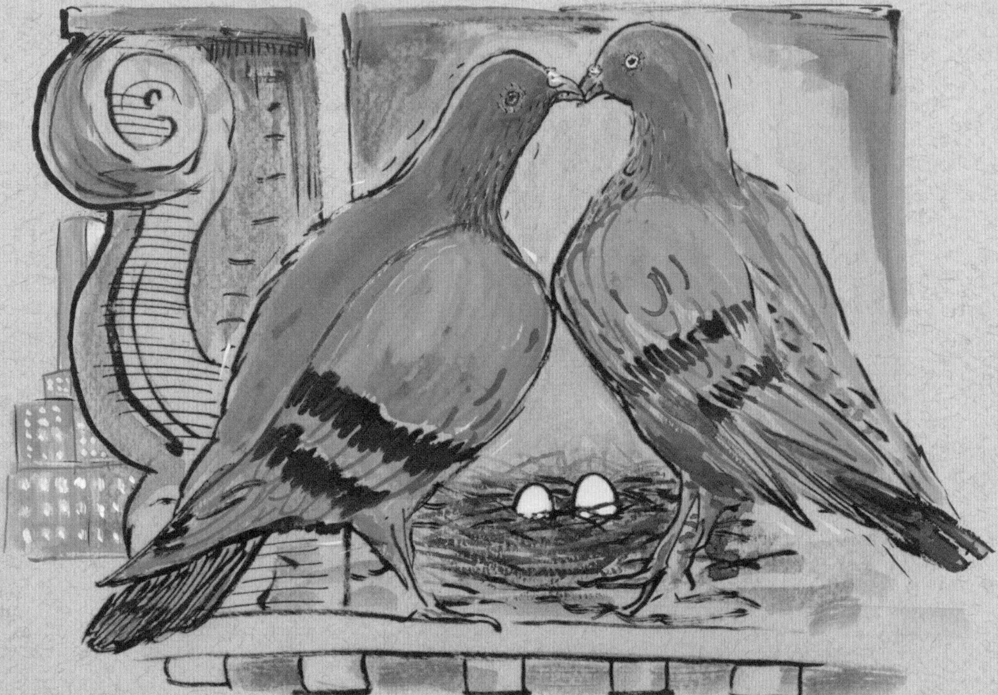

PIGEONS MATE FOR LIFE.

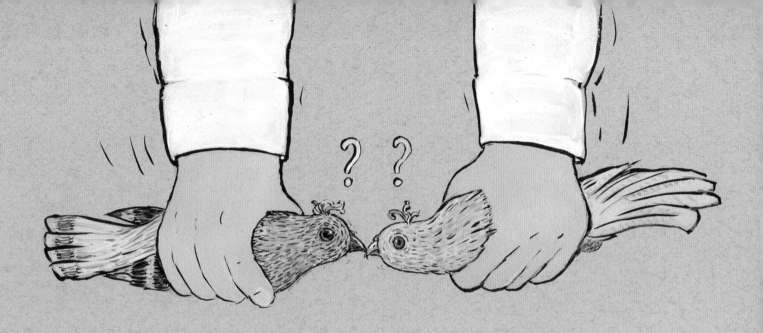

IF A HUMAN PICKS THE TWO
PIGEONS TO MATE, THAT IS CALLED
BREEDING.

BREEDERS MAKE SOME STRANGE BIRDS!

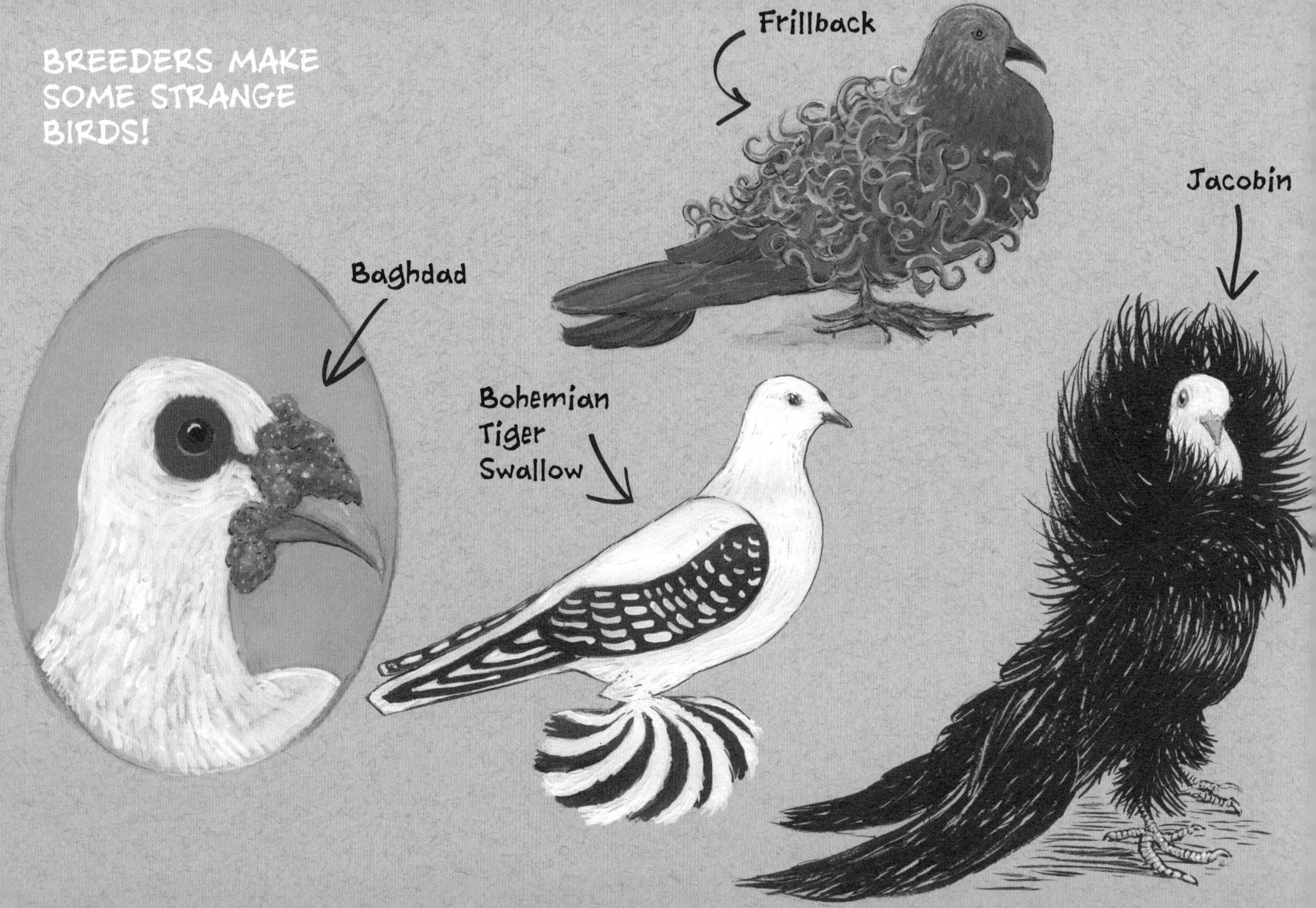
Frillback
Jacobin
Baghdad
Bohemian Tiger Swallow

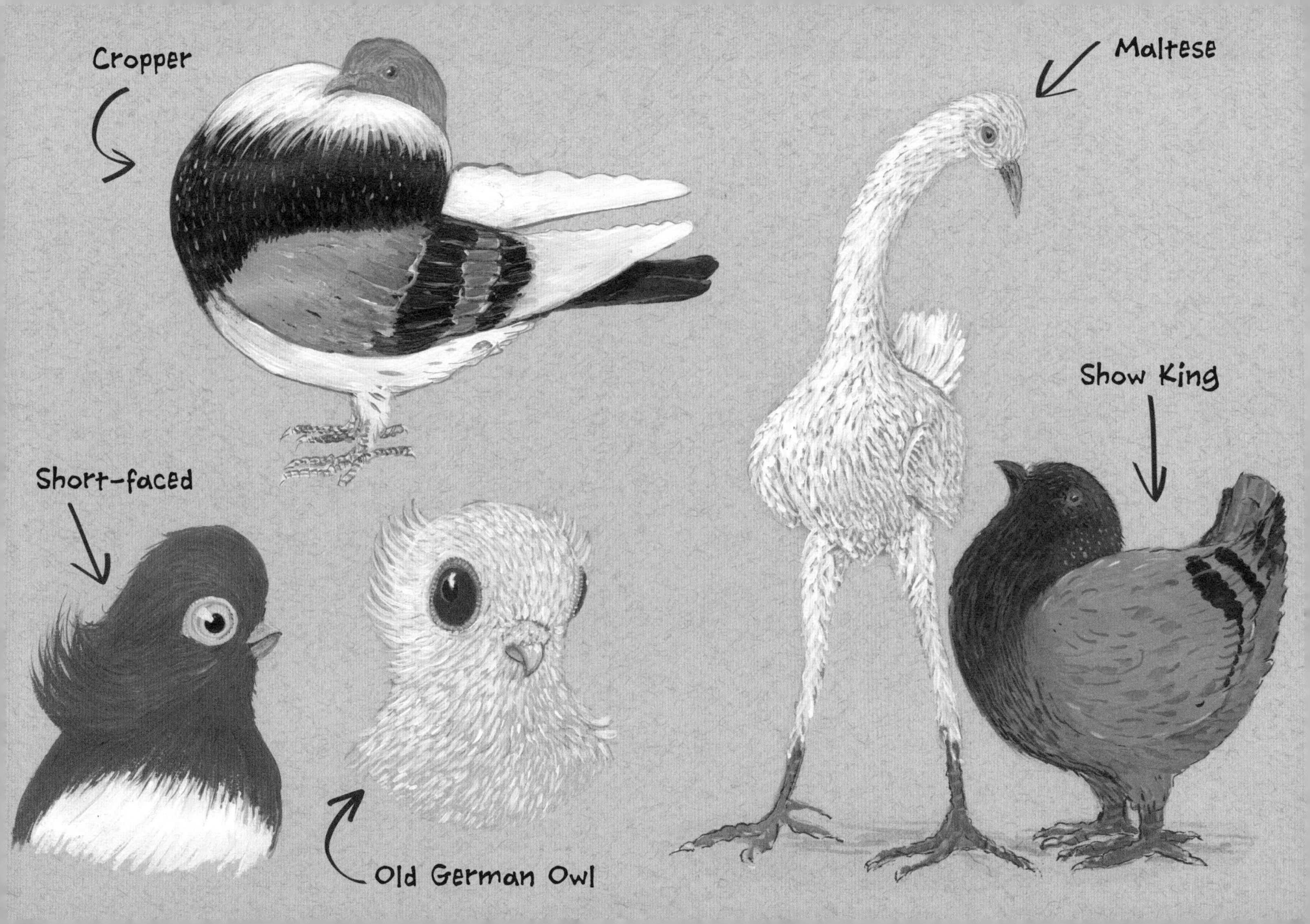
Cropper
Maltese
Show King
Short-faced
Old German Owl

THE FANTAIL
IS A
PRETTY
PIGEON.

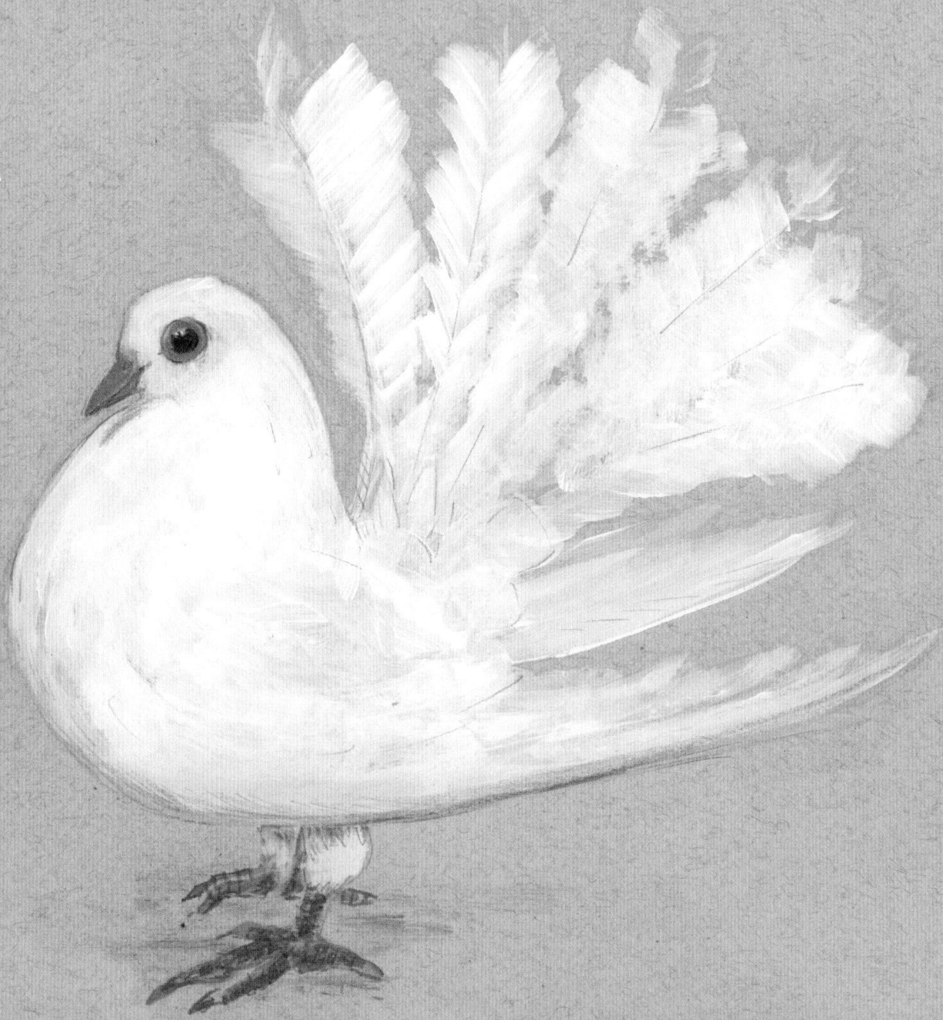

FANCIES
ARE PIGEONS
THAT LOOK
FANCY!

THE VICTORIA CROWNED
IS THE **BIGGEST**
LIVING PIGEON.

IT IS NAMED FOR
QUEEN VICTORIA
OF ENGLAND.

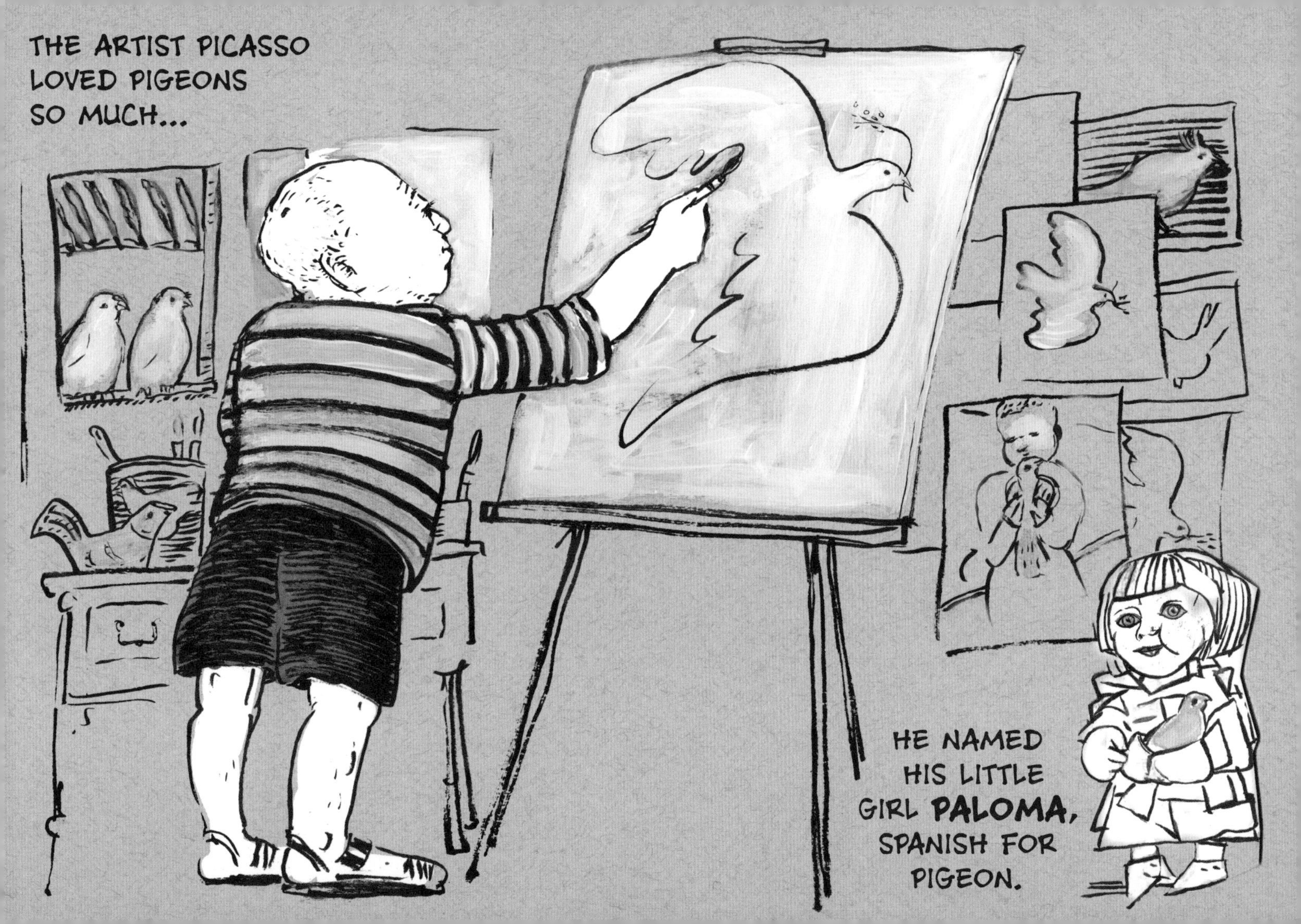
THE ARTIST PICASSO LOVED PIGEONS SO MUCH...
HE NAMED HIS LITTLE GIRL **PALOMA**, SPANISH FOR PIGEON.

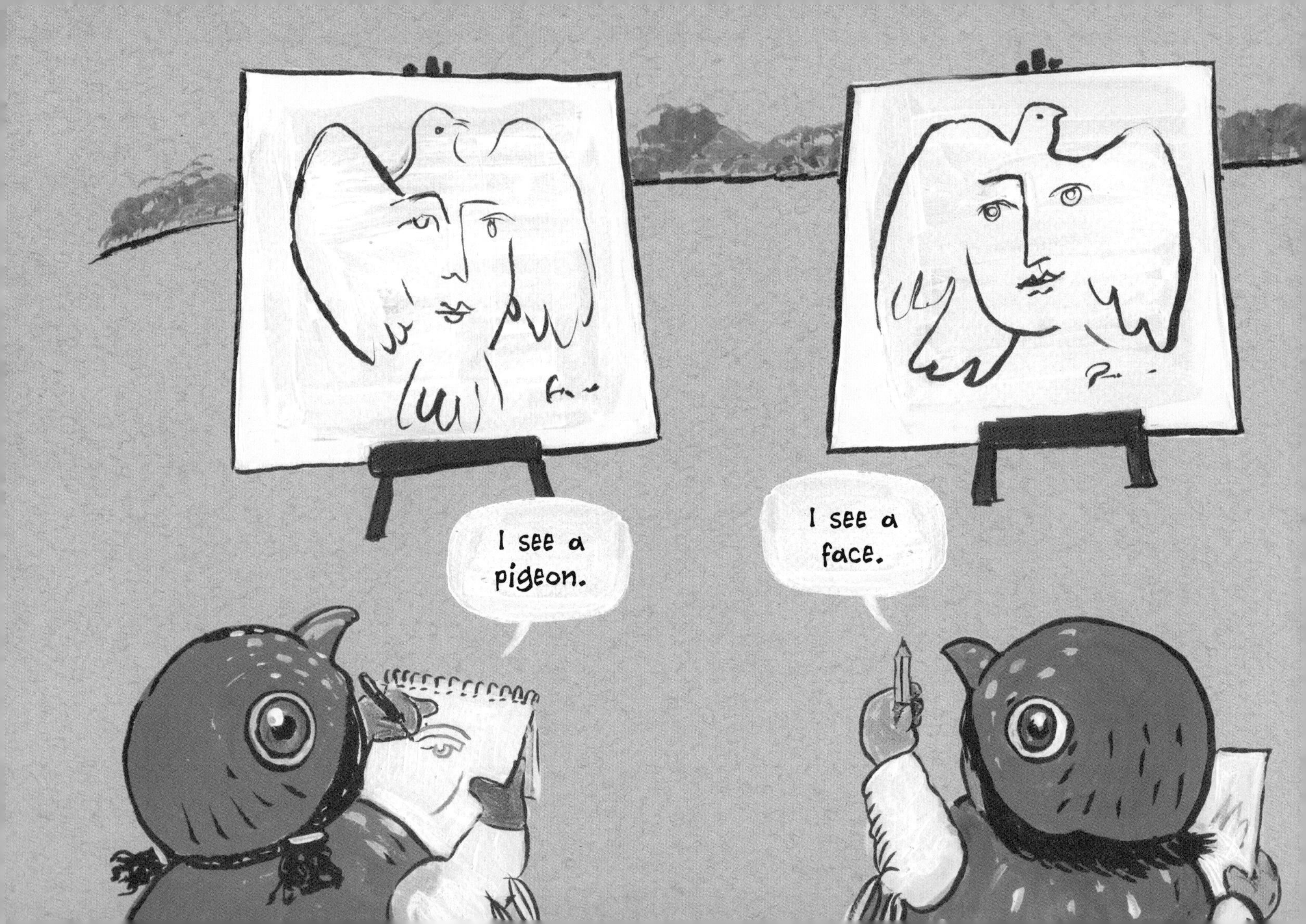
I see a pigeon.
I see a face.

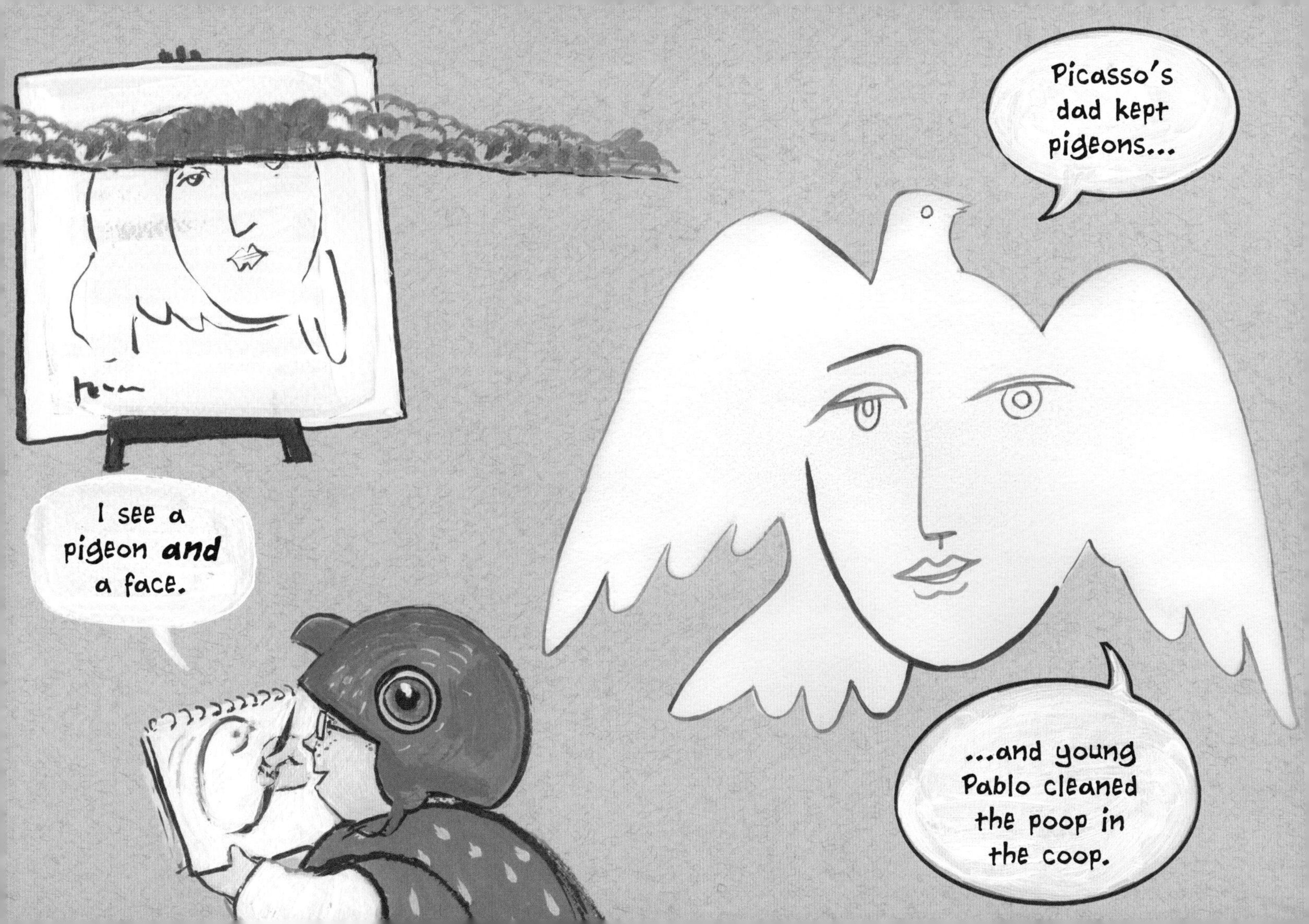
Picasso's dad kept pigeons...
...and young Pablo cleaned the poop in the coop.
I see a pigeon **and** a face.

SOME PIGEONS CAN BE **VERY** BIG. THE **DODO** WAS THREE FEET TALL.

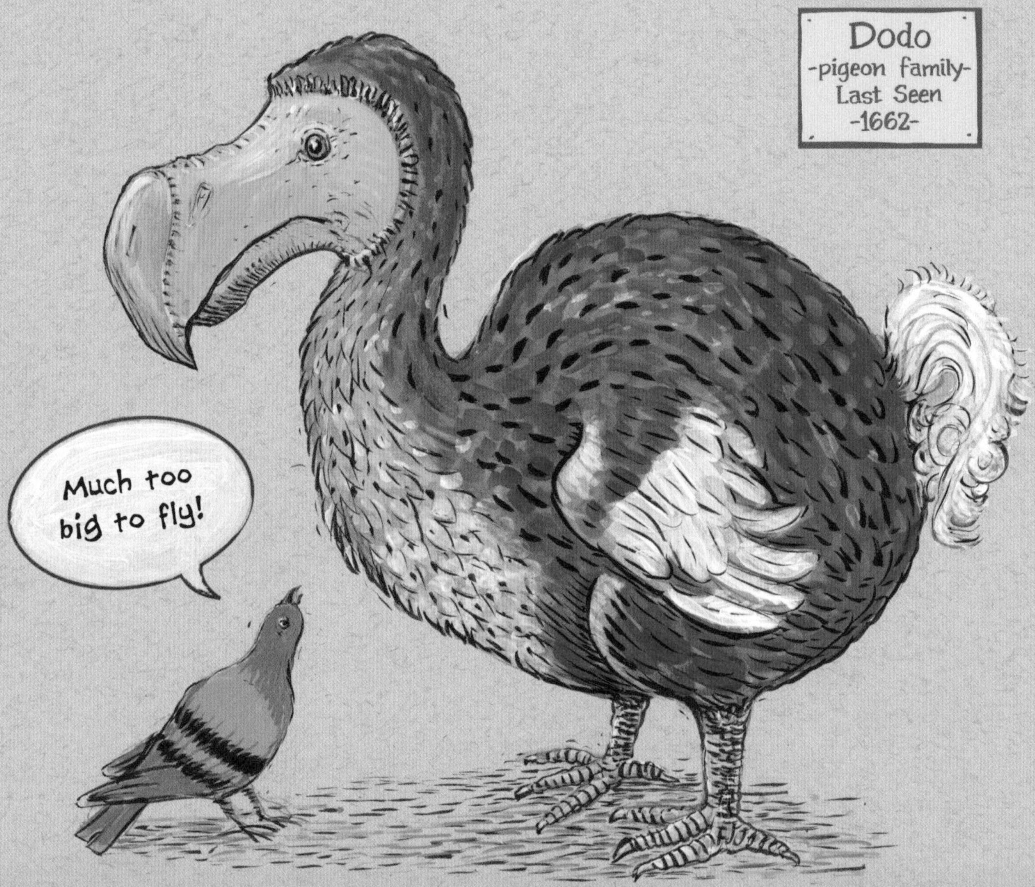

Dodo
-pigeon family-
Last Seen
-1662-
Much too big to fly!

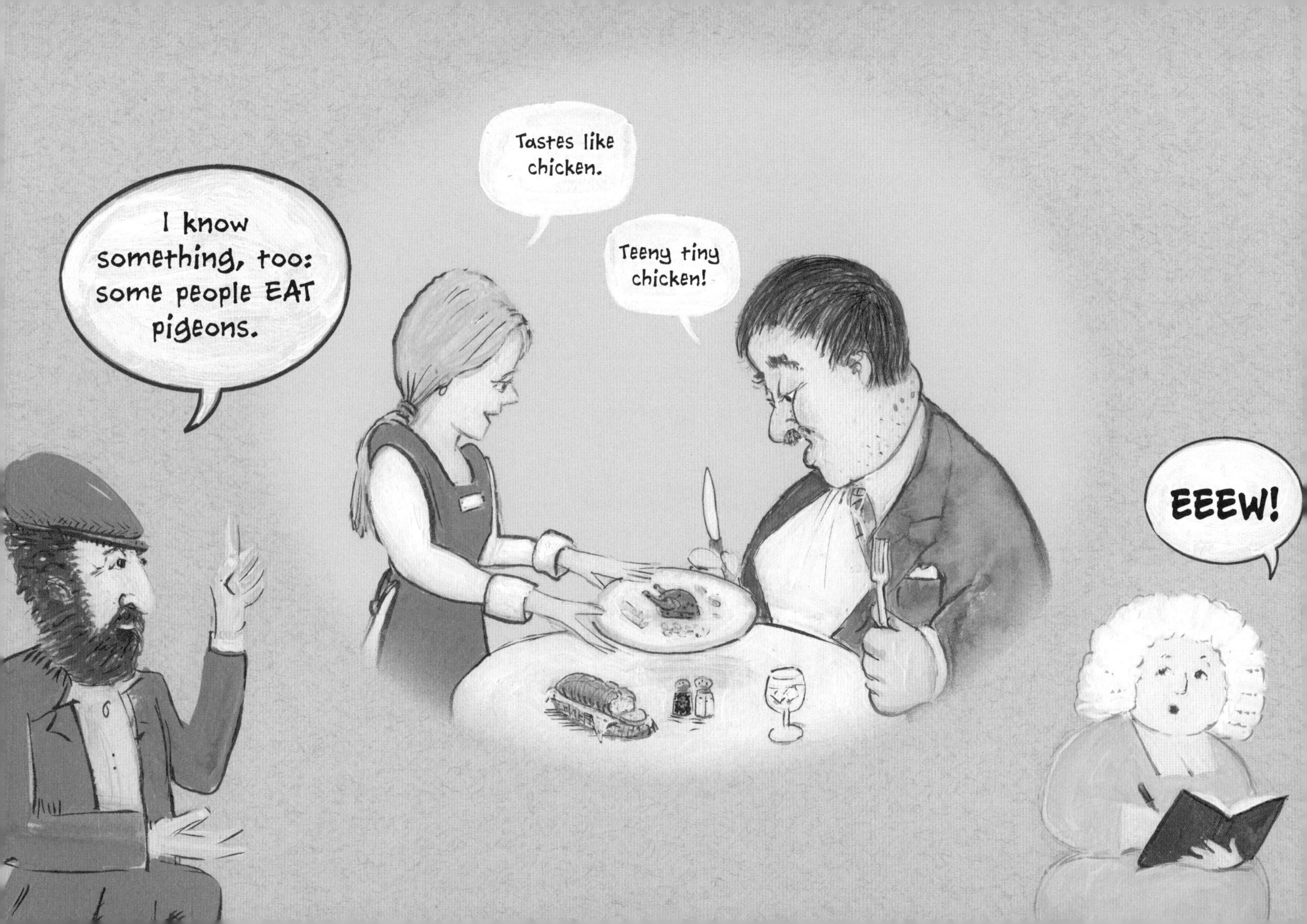
I know something, too: some people EAT pigeons.
Tastes like chicken.
Teeny tiny chicken!
EEEW!

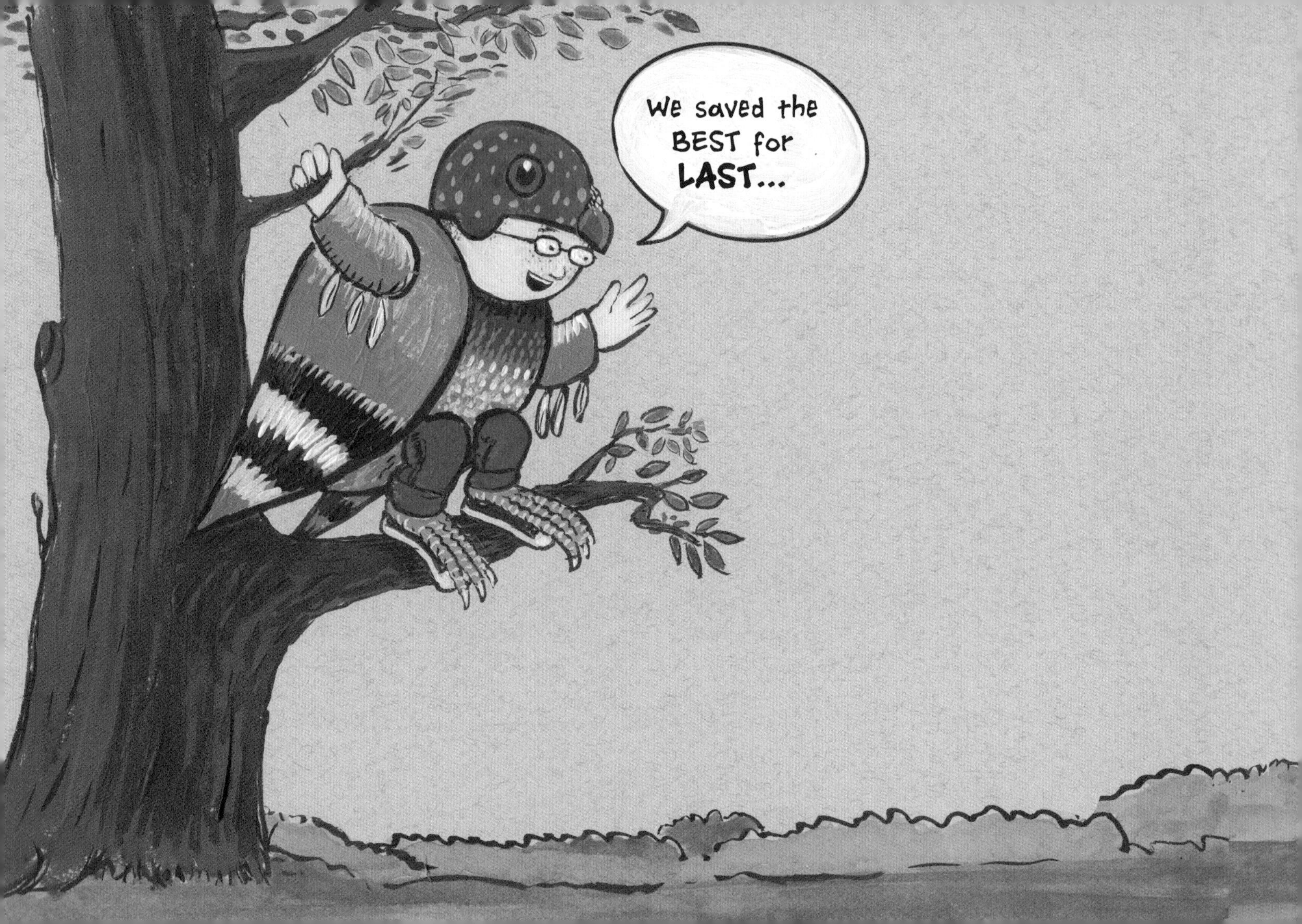
We saved the BEST for LAST...

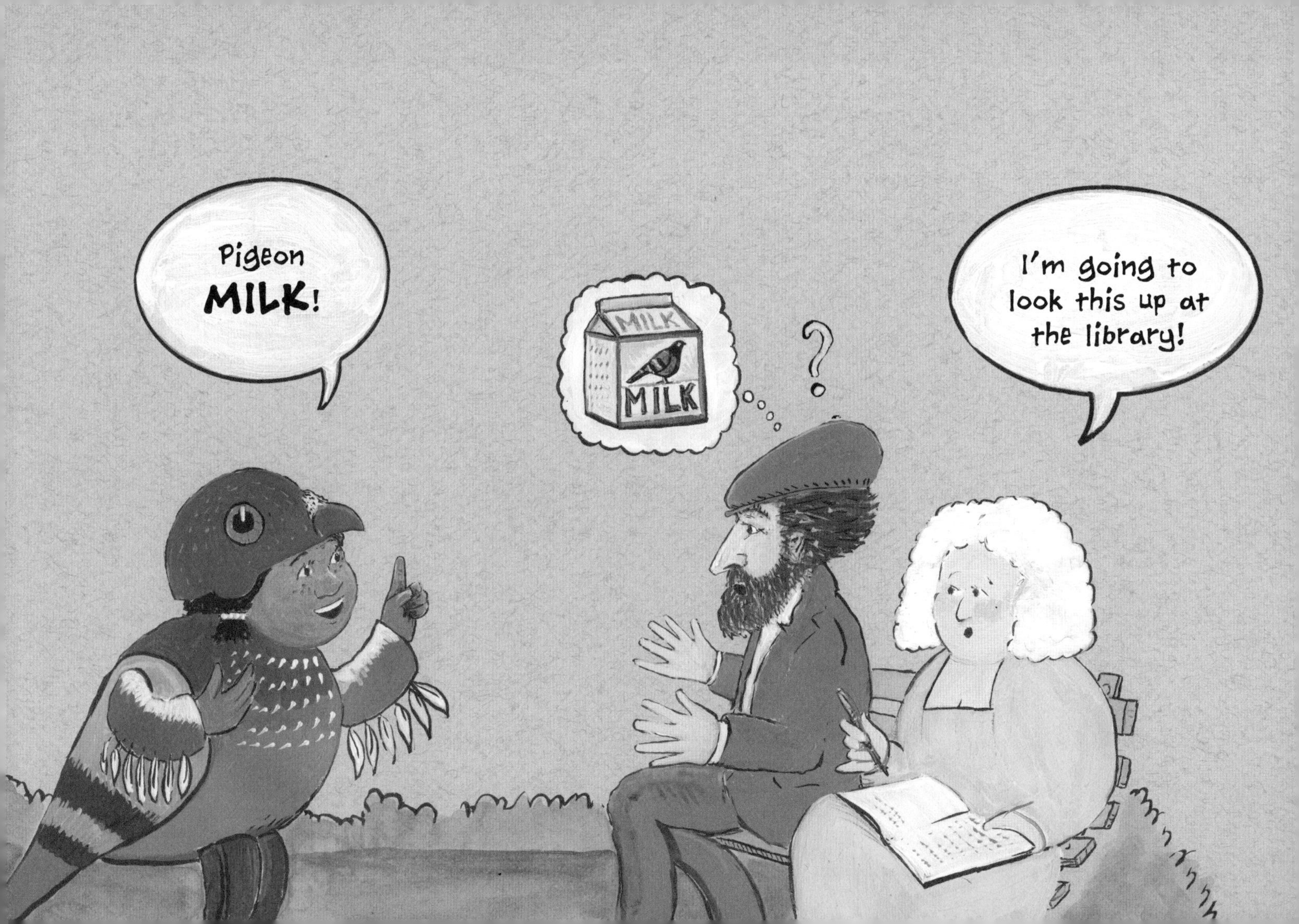
Pigeon MILK!
MILK
MILK
?
I'm going to look this up at the library!

PIGEON MILK DOES **NOT** COME FROM A MOTHER'S BREAST.

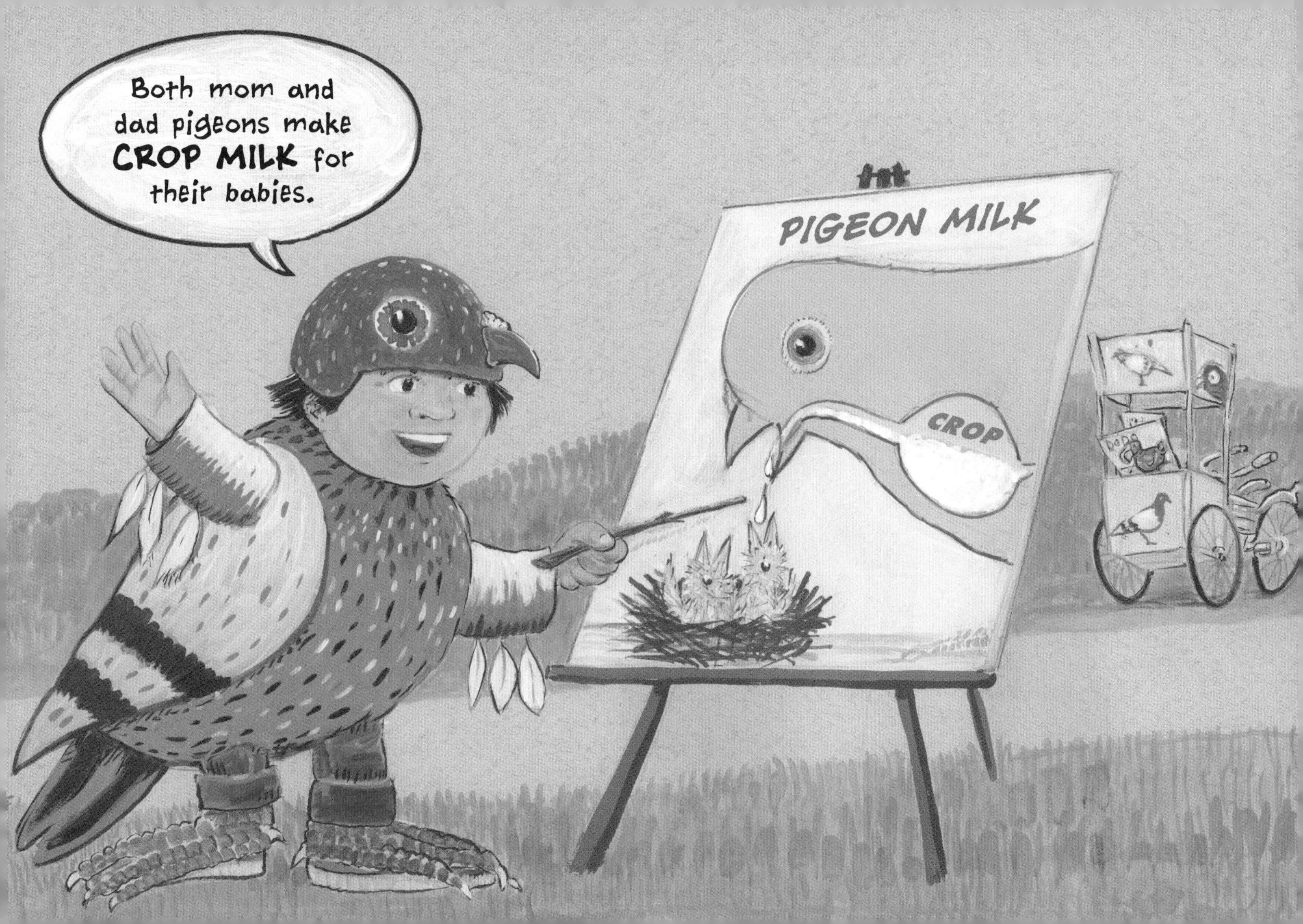
Both mom and dad pigeons make **CROP MILK** for their babies.
PIGEON MILK
CROP

A FEW OTHER BIRDS MAKE CROP MILK FOR THEIR CHICKS.

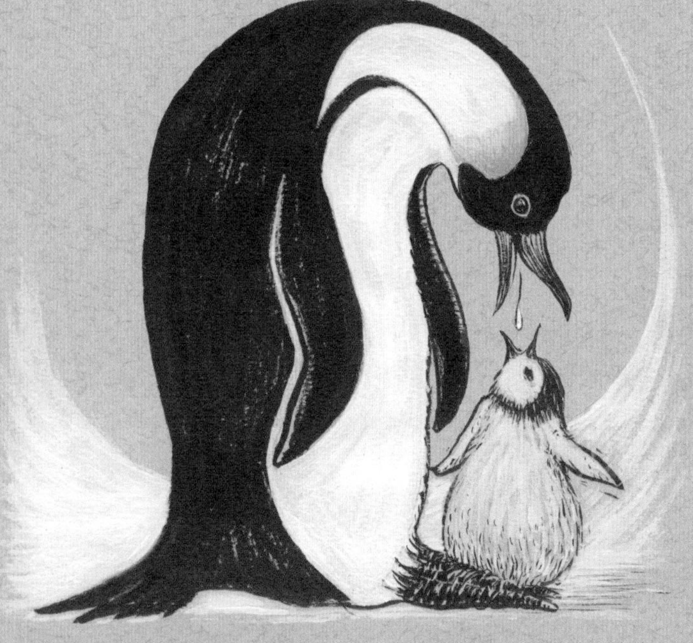

EMPEROR PENGUINS

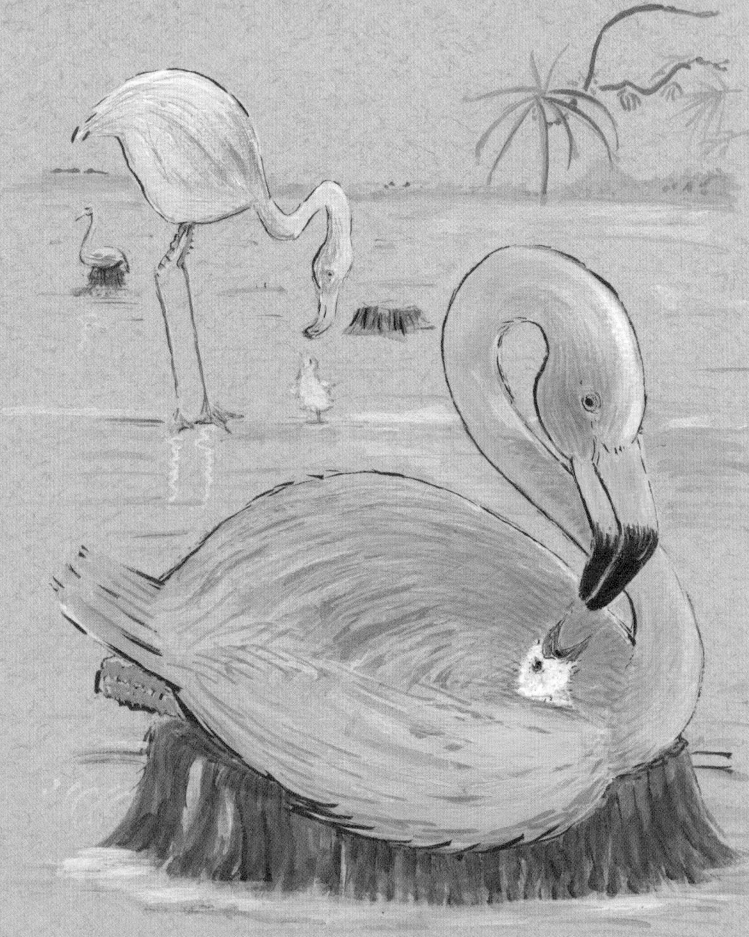

FLAMINGOS

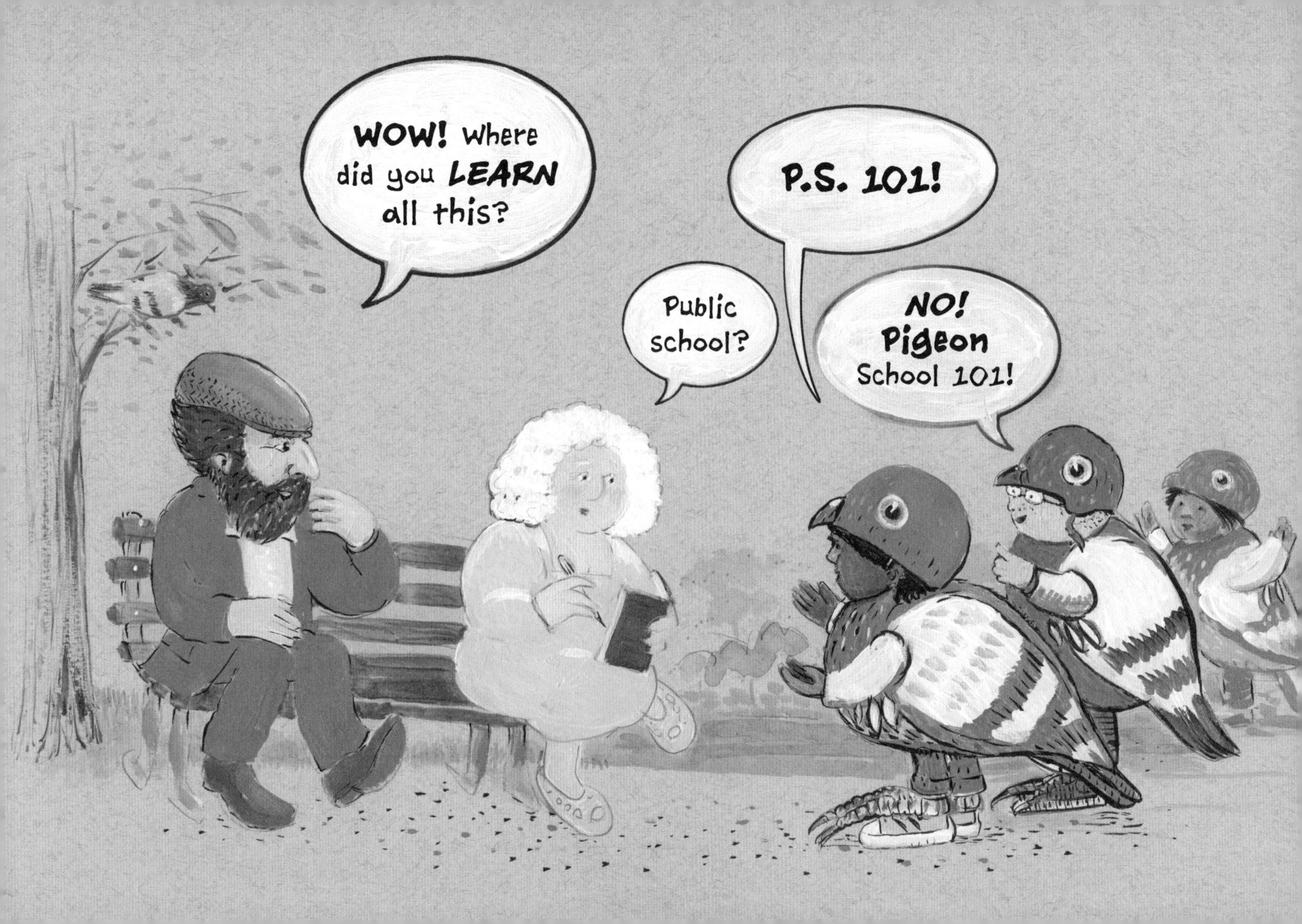
WOW! Where did you LEARN all this?
Public school?
P.S. 101!
NO! Pigeon School 101!

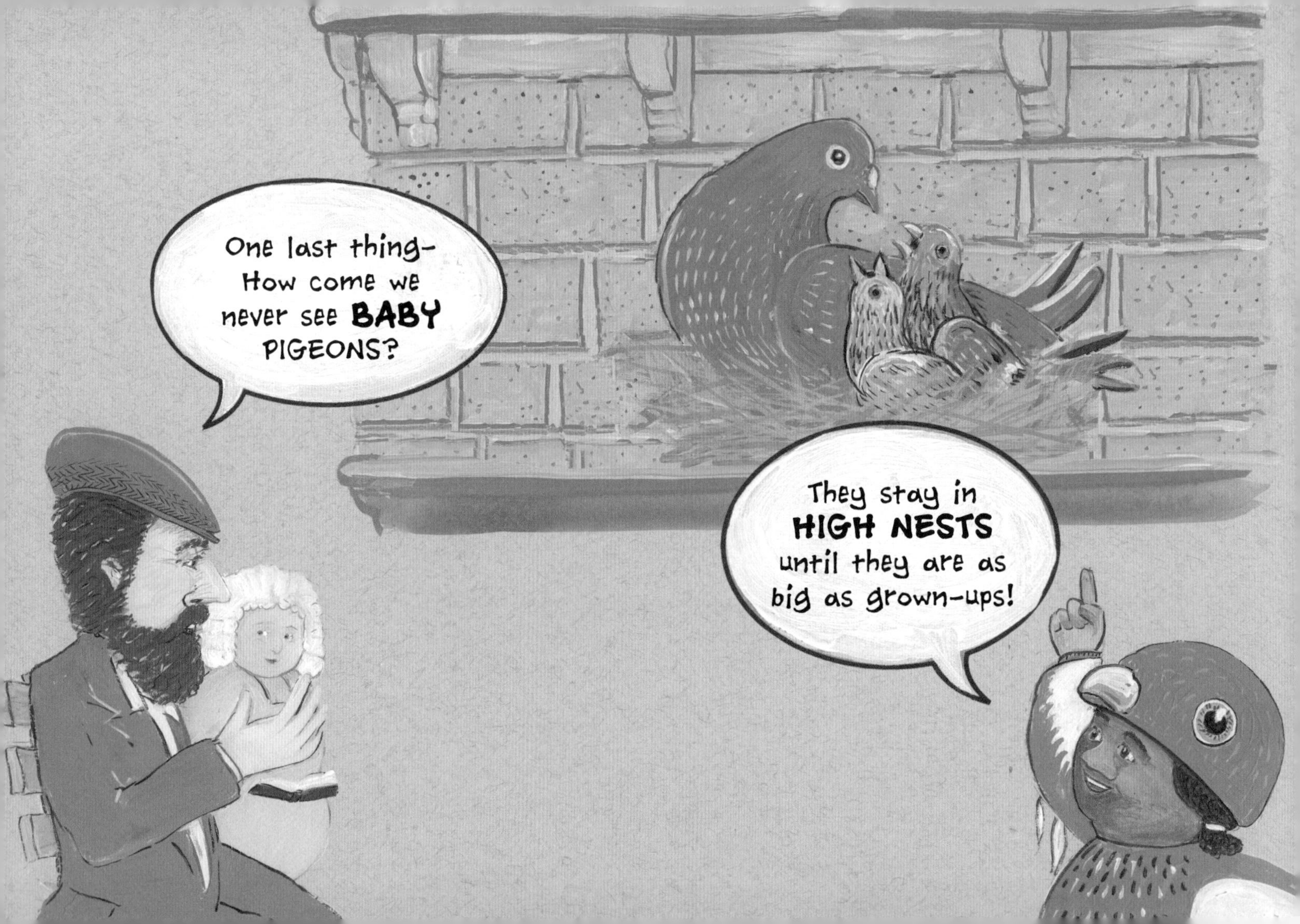
One last thing- How come we never see BABY PIGEONS?
They stay in HIGH NESTS until they are as big as grown-ups!

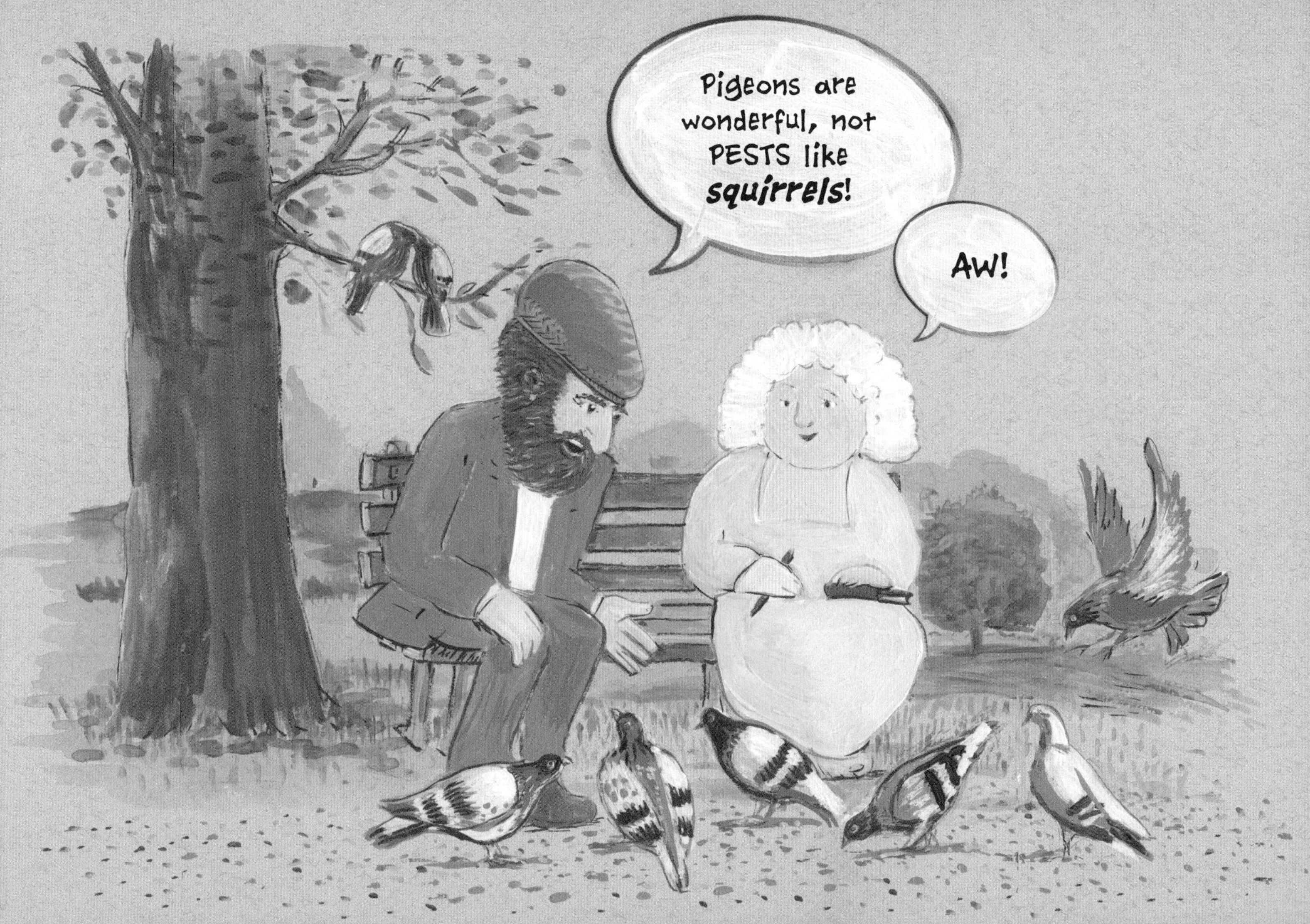
Pigeons are wonderful, not PESTS like ***squirrels***!
AW!

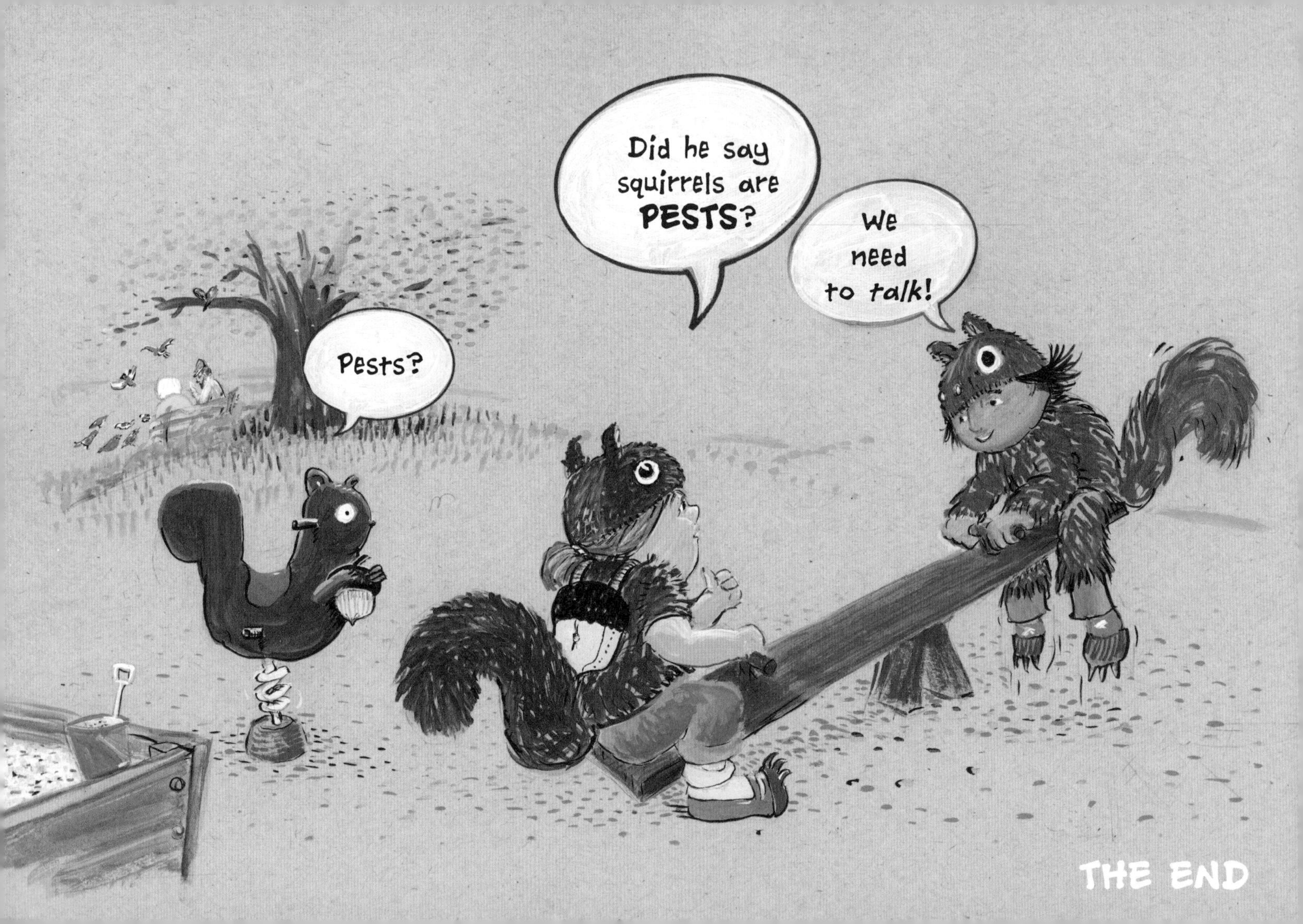
Pests?
Did he say squirrels are PESTS?
We need to talk!
THE END